H2O

Jane Martin

A SAMUEL FRENCH ACTING EDITION

SAMUEL FRENCH

FOUNDED 1830

SAMUELFRENCH.COM
SAMUELFRENCH-LONDON.CO.UK

ISBN 978-0-573-70302-7

www.SamuelFrench.com
www.SamuelFrench-London.co.uk

FOR PRODUCTION ENQUIRIES

UNITED STATES AND CANADA
Info@SamuelFrench.com
1-866-598-8449

UNITED KINGDOM AND EUROPE
Plays@SamuelFrench-London.co.uk
020-7255-4302

Each title is subject to availability from Samuel French, depending upon country of performance. Please be aware that *H2O* may not be licensed by Samuel French in your territory. Professional and amateur producers should contact the nearest Samuel French office or licensing partner to verify availability.

MUSIC USE NOTE

Licensees are solely responsible for obtaining formal written permission from copyright owners to use copyrighted music in the performance of this play and are strongly cautioned to do so. If no such permission is obtained by the licensee, then the licensee must use only original music that the licensee owns and controls. Licensees are solely responsible and liable for all music clearances and shall indemnify the copyright owners of the play(s) and their licensing agent, Samuel French, against any costs, expenses, losses and liabilities arising from the use of music by licensees. Please contact the appropriate music licensing authority in your territory for the rights to any incidental music.

IMPORTANT BILLING AND CREDIT REQUIREMENTS

If you have obtained performance rights to this title, please refer to your licensing agreement for important billing and credit requirements.

H2O was first produced by the Contemporary American Theatre Festival at Shepherd University in Shepherdstown, West Virginia on July 5, 2013. The performance was directed by Jon Jory, with sets by David M. Barber, costumes by Margaret A. McKowen, lighting by John Ambrosone, and sound by Christina Smith. The Production Stage Manager was Debre A. Acquavella. The cast was as follows:

DEBORAH... Diane Mair
JAKE ....Alex Podulke

CHARACTERS

DEBORAH

JAKE

SETTING

New York City.

TIME

The present.

For Ed Herendeen

ACT ONE

Scene One – Jake's Apartment

(The play takes place on an open stage against a cyc. Place is changed simply with furniture and light. Eight scene and costume changers are necessary for au vista work during the play. All the play's action takes place in New York City. The play begins with a bare stage. A young woman walks downstage to talk to us. She carries her shoulder bag.)

DEBORAH. Actually, Jesus doesn't have much to say about actresses. Early Christians were Simon and his brother, Andrew, were fisherman. John and James, son of Zebediah the same. Mathew was a tax collector. The rest of the disciples, who knows but I don't think they were in the arts. Jesus spoke to me and told me acting was my service and my way. I was in the New York Public Library looking at a first folio of Shakespeare's and...

(The stage is set with an air mattress, a duffel bag, a wooden chair, a rolling bathroom door, a rolling apartment door, and several resume photographs of actresses.)

God spoke to me...well...No, it wasn't a voice exactly but it was clear and decisive, "I am the Son of David and this work you must continue". Period, end. God's will, Wednesday, October Nineteenth, two ten p.m. 2008. So I do. I continue.

(She moves off. A man in his late 30's dressed in a shirt and jeans, barefooted moves down to address us.)

JAKE. A guy goes into a bar and orders three whiskies. Drinks all three. Does this day after day. Bartender says, "Listen pal, I can put all three shots in one glass for you." The guy says, "I have two brothers in Armenia, Dikran and Garabed, this way I can feel like I'm home, drinking with them." Couple months later he comes in, only orders two shots...

(Takes a knife out of a leather holster on the jeans)

Bartender looks up, says, "Whatsa matter, somethin' happen to one of your brothers?"

(Pulls the knife across one of his wrists. We see blood.)

Guy says, "No, they're fine..."

(Changes hands and cuts the other wrist)

I just quit drinking.

(Looks at audience)

Tough house.

(He exits. The woman, DEBORAH, enters. She knocks on downstage door.)

DEBORAH. Mr. Abadjian?

(No answer. She knocks again.)

Mr. Abadjian? It's Deborah Elling. I'm your four o'clock.

JAKE. *(Offstage)* Fuck that burns.

DEBORAH. What? *(Opens door)* Mr. Abadjian?

(Steps in)

Your four o'clock audition.

(He enters from bathroom. Blood on his chest and heavily on his arms and hands.)

JAKE. Who are you?

DEBORAH. Dear Jesus.

JAKE. Can't see.

(He falls to the floor unconscious. She throws her shoulder bag on the floor and paws through it looking for her phone.)

DEBORAH. Mr. Abadjian?

(Finds phone)

Oh my Lord. Ok...

(Calls 911)

Yes, ummmm...there's a...a man badly injured at... Blood on his arms and chest he...wrists...ummm, I don't think so...I can't find a pulse but...yes...I'm sorry...4 4... I'm sorry...I'm a blank...

(Finds paper)

Here...it's 448 W. 124th Street, Apartment 4C...48... you better...wait...

(Hands on his chest)

Breathing, yes... he uh...I'm pretty sure he... Oh God, cut his wrist...no... Mr. Abadjian...no...not talking... not responding...Deborah Elling...Elling...Not a friend just...How would I do that?

(Looking back)

A strap thing... blood flow. Right. Yes. I can let you in. Yes.

(Disconnects. Grabs an elastic strap from her stuff and starts to do a tourniquet.)

Heavenly Father, First by virtue of creation, Second by virtue of regeneration, third by virtue of your person...

*(Lights fade. **DEBORAH** moves down to audience, Stage is cleared. A stool is placed downstage for her.)*

Scene Two – Hospital

DEBORAH. *(Speaks to audience.)* World ministries or Covenant of Christ Alive that's my church, My Father's Church in Fayette, Missouri…sometimes in New York. Back and forth like the old mule ministries. Ummm… if you were interested…in joining…we uh… We would only ask two questions: do you confess Jesus Christ as your savior and promise to follow him as Lord? That would be one…the other: Do you accept the Holy Scriptures, the Old and New Testaments, as the word of God and the only perfect rule for faith, doctrine and conduct? Just those. No, what I do is not in conflict with my faith. That's a misunderstanding. Yes, I could play a prostitute but I would not…would not remove my… Yes, I could swear if the character were in some way… redeemed, or if her frailty… if it was…

*(The stool is struck and a hospital bed set. **JAKE** is in the bed with a hospital gown on. Chair is placed by bed. Lights up on **JAKE** in the hospital bed sleeping. His wrists are bandaged. **DEBORAH** kneels and prays quietly near the bed. He wakes and props himself up to look at her.)*

Thou, Lord, art my Redeemer and my strength. I ask of you, oh, Lord, allow me Lord to heal those who have been torn…

JAKE. Well, this is fucked.

DEBORAH. *(Startled)* Oh.

JAKE. Yeah, 'Oh.'

DEBORAH. I'm…

JAKE. You weren't…I… Wait…You're the one, right? You?

DEBORAH. The one who…

JAKE. Yeah. Yeah, you.

DEBORAH. I…

JAKE. And now you're…

DEBORAH. I had the…

JAKE. Here.

DEBORAH. Four o'clock...

JAKE. Unfucking believable.

DEBORAH. I was supposed to...

JAKE. Wait.

DEBORAH. Audition for...

JAKE. Shut up.

DEBORAH. Ophelia.

> *(He lies back down. A pause. She comes and tentatively sits in the chair by his bed.)*

JAKE. Were you praying?

DEBORAH. Mr. Abadjian...

JAKE. Over there...

DEBORAH. I was...

JAKE. On the floor. Were you praying?

DEBORAH. I was, yes.

JAKE. *(He laughs.)* Ow. Shit, that hurts.

DEBORAH. I should go, I...

JAKE. No. All right... This is actually...

DEBORAH. I just came by...

JAKE. You came by?

DEBORAH. Yes.

JAKE. What the hell is your name?

DEBORAH. Deborah Elling.

JAKE. You came by for what?

DEBORAH. To see if...

JAKE. To pray on the floor?

DEBORAH. No, I...

JAKE. You called 911, right?

DEBORAH. You were...bleeding...and I...

JAKE. Yeah, I know that.

DEBORAH. I should...

JAKE. Sit the fuck down!

DEBORAH. *(Not moving)* Watch your mouth.

JAKE. Oh. Okay Ellen…

DEBORAH. Deborah.

JAKE. DEBORAH. I certainly wouldn't want to fucking offend you.

(She starts out.)

I wanted to die is that clear? That was not, Deborah, a 'cry for help', okay? You know, all those phrases, I hate shit like that. I like to be taken at face value. I am not complex. I cut my wrists to get this over with. So as to be nothing. So, for one thing, I would not wake up in a hospital and find someone praying for me. But you, who knew me not at all, who understood nothing…wait…you had seen me in the movies, right? Dawnwalker. The super hero who only saves humanity from first light to sunrise… You're a fan, right Deborah?

DEBORAH. No.

JAKE. And on this basis you decided to save the one thing I didn't want, my fucking life and then worse, worse, to show up here to what? Receive my gratitude, is that it? Well, okay, you don't have my gratitude, Deborah, you and your praying and the fact you decided to show up here…you and who? Your Christ? Unbelievable. Hey, Deborah, take your fairy tales and your charmless, gullible nature and get the hell out of my room.

DEBORAH. No.

JAKE. No??

DEBORAH. I'll sit with you for a while.

JAKE. I don't want you to sit with me.

DEBORAH. We don't always get what we want.

JAKE. Are you a stalker, Deborah?

DEBORAH. No, I don't find you attractive.

JAKE. But you find me what?

DEBORAH. Touching.

JAKE. Really? Why am I touching?

DEBORAH. Because you are drained of meaning.

(The lights change. Hospital bed and chair struck. **JAKE** *speaks to audience taking off his hospital gown.* **JAKE***'s apartment door, wooden chair, mattress are set.)*

Scene Three – Jake's Apartment

JAKE. Dude, in New York City they arrest you for attempted suicide. Really. Anyway they're taking me out to Rikers in the ambulance and the EMS guy says, "Damn man you're Dawnwalker, right? Louis, this guys a fuckin' movie star! Yo, gimme your autograph, okay?" So I ask him does he have a pen? and he says "Fuck that, man, dip your fingers in your blood and write it on my whites, dude." Then these guys laugh like lunatics. Dip your finger in your blood, right?

(He is back in his apartment. He exercises. Deborah knocks.)

JAKE. Yeah.

DEBORAH. Deborah Elling.

(A pause)

JAKE. It's unlocked.

DEBORAH. Hi.

JAKE. Hi.

DEBORAH. I think there's a misunderstanding.

JAKE. What would that be?

DEBORAH. I received a phone call from Alexander Basy.

JAKE. *(Back to exercising)* Yeah, he's producing Hamlet.

DEBORAH. Would you mind not doing that?

JAKE. Finishing a set. *(He does.)* What?

DEBORAH. He says I'm cast as Ophelia in your production of Hamlet.

JAKE. *(Swigging from a quart water bottle)* Yeah? And?

DEBORAH. You are a…

JAKE. *(Nodding)* Right…

DEBORAH. I don't think it…

JAKE. *(Kicking the one chair towards her)* Take a pew.

DEBORAH. happens without you.

JAKE. Alex is the producer ok?

DEBORAH. *(About the chair)* No thank you.

JAKE. Sit.

DEBORAH. I didn't audition for Ophelia.

JAKE. Microwaved coffee?

DEBORAH. We didn't get that far.

JAKE. How far is that?

DEBORAH. An audition…

JAKE. As if I really wanted to know…

DEBORAH. because you…

JAKE. Just sit, okay?!

(Puts her in chair)

DEBORAH. Please don't touch me.

JAKE. Yeah, right.

DEBORAH. So I could not possibly.

JAKE. Relax, Deborah, or I will kill myself.

DEBORAH. That is not funny in the least.

JAKE. We have a substantially different sense of humor.

DEBORAH. I don't…

JAKE. Shhh. Breathe.

DEBORAH. I…

JAKE. Breathe.

(A pause. They breathe.)

Good, more.

(Silence)

DEBORAH. I should have asked if you're feeling better.

JAKE. And I should have…Okay, I owe you…you mind if I have *coffee?*

DEBORAH. You don't have to…

JAKE. I do. Yeah. I want to…All right, for this moment, now it seems better, or ummm, useful, not to be dead. Why? I have no idea, Deborah, I can't…umm, The 911 call, thank you for that. Ummm.

DEBORAH. It was…This is…

JAKE. Fucking awkward.

DEBORAH. Please…

JAKE. Sorry. Awkward, no modifier.

DEBORAH. It's not my business but…

JAKE. No, it's not your business.

DEBORAH. I shouldn't have…

JAKE. Shhh.

DEBORAH. I…

JAKE. I'm a fucking mess, Deborah. This might have occurred to you. Assfuckistan, my girlfriend gets a double mastectomy and those were my favorite parts, my father fucks up his brother… I'm an alcoholic and my dog dies. Wait. These are just the funny stuff… Just events. I get out of jail, which had something to do with throwing no left turn-signs set in buckets of concrete through store windows. I catch a ride to LA with some buddies, play music, work for an escort service, roll a couple of drunks and two months later I'm Dawnwalker, the super hero who never speaks, do two sequels and make thirty million dollars, sleep with three hundred women and I am so ridiculous, such a joke, I kill myself and you screw it up. Even talking about it is ridiculous.

DEBORAH. I didn't ask.

JAKE. You mean I brought it up?

DEBORAH. You did.

JAKE. Now I wish I was dead.

DEBORAH. Mr. Abadjian…

JAKE. Jake.

DEBORAH. Mr. Abadjian…

JAKE. Jake.

DEBORAH. I don't want Ophelia, Jake, if it's just…

JAKE. A mercy fuck?

DEBORAH. I have asked you not to… yes. I have to go.

JAKE. You want to earn it, deserve it?

DEBORAH. I do, yes.

(She starts to go.)

JAKE. That is so fucked up. I'm supposed to listen to your ninety seconds of Shakespeare and then you would deserve it? Acting's a farce, Deborah, a shuck, a shell game, so lighten up a little and get down in the mud with the rest of us.

(She slings her shoulder bag at him.)

DEBORAH. Excuse me…

JAKE. Whoa, Whoa, Whoa.

DEBORAH. I'm not in a farce, Jake. Sorry. I am in my life in God's service. I've been in New York for four years and I have done eleven Shakespeare's in parks, and parking lots and prisons and an abandoned hospital and I have never gotten more than bus fare, so my story is a little different than yours. Until two months ago I lived with seventeen women in the dormitory of a Christian hostel. I have seventy dollars in checking and nine dollars in my bag. You think you're a joke? I won't do plays that don't enable God's handiwork, now let's see you make a career out of that? Oh, and I don't take handouts. You want an argument for the existence of God, try Shakespeare.

JAKE. Yeah, got it.

DEBORAH. He transcends man while showing what man could be. Which by the way, Mr. Abadjian, you don't. So despite the fact I would commit…sins…to play opposite Dawnwalker, because everybody who is anybody will come to gawk at you, and I will blow them away and have an actual career that I can use to fill my heart and bring people to Christ. But I'm not going to demean my talent and purpose so you can feel better about your infinite confusion and wasteful life.

JAKE. What sins would you commit?

DEBORAH. You are unbelievable. *(She starts to exit apartment.)*

JAKE. Very poetic, very heart felt, the perils of being Christian, right?

DEBORAH. *(Returns)* Go on.

JAKE. Look, I need help, okay and you seem… I don't know…addicted to helping, plus you seem like a complete victim…

DEBORAH. I am not a…

JAKE. And what could be better for Ophelia? So help me out and do the play, alright? I've never done a play.

DEBORAH. So you're starting with Hamlet?

JAKE. Nice instinct for the jugular. I am, yes, because…

DEBORAH. You can.

JAKE. Yes. No.

DEBORAH. Yes.

JAKE. *(Deadly serious)* Deborah, I'm nothing…like you said in the hospital and nothing, Deborah, kills itself. Hamlet is like a…a massive something, right? Plus he starts out suicidal and ends up…

DEBORAH. Dead.

JAKE. For something.

DEBORAH. Honor.

JAKE. I could be down with that. Help 'nobody' out here.

DEBORAH. A recent poll shows that you have better name recognition than Buddha, Vishnu and Ghandi.

JAKE. But I lose to Christ, right?

DEBORAH. You do, yes.

JAKE. Look, I have casting approval for Ophelia and Gertrude.

DEBORAH. Because of the above.

JAKE. No, because that's where all the emotion lives for him. With the guys it's just anger and confusion. I can, believe me, do that.

DEBORAH. And I could help you how?

JAKE. Language, for one. I'm scared of the language, and…

DEBORAH. And?

JAKE. You fuckin' wind me up.

DEBORAH. And?

JAKE. You would know me.

DEBORAH. I don't know you.

JAKE. It just matters that I think you do. I came from a town of four hundred people. Anything I did I did with people who knew me. They are bringing in big time British actor-elephants for this. I need to know somebody.

(A pause)

DEBORAH. May I call you Jake?

JAKE. No. I'm kidding.

DEBORAH. You're a little old for a babysitter, Jake.

JAKE. Nice.

DEBORAH. May I tell you what I know about you?

JAKE. Maybe.

DEBORAH. Because what I know about you I don't much like.

JAKE. Okay.

DEBORAH. You're a masochist and a narcissist.

JAKE. But I'm cute, right?

DEBORAH. *(Not giving an inch)* Yes, you're cute.

JAKE. Your categories?

DEBORAH. Yes.

JAKE. Who wants me to be anything else? Conceive this, okay, I get anything I want. I'm filming in Witches Nipple, Utah and I want fresh blowfish sushi for lunch that gets flown in. Women? I'm a tourist destination, Deborah. I shop they don't ask me to pay. Money, okay, is completely devalued. Any impulse I have is rewarded. I am clearly the center of the universe. And the joke is, if you have no boundaries you don't exist. And you know what? Fuck that.

DEBORAH. That's a really sad story.

JAKE. That's a really cheap response.

DEBORAH. Maybe you can hear this. I'm not the center of the known universe. I made seven hundred dollars as an actress last year. I play High Schools, scummy parks, ninety seat theatres and I'm really good and I don't allow it to be demeaned...

JAKE. Yeah, fine.

DEBORAH. And the fact, as far as you let me see, that you allow everything to be demeaned is what my Dad calls 'soul-sickness' and I can tell you the spiritual answer is Christ and the Temporal answer, for me, is Shakespeare- the beauty he makes out of the mess we're in. So I find it infuriating that you offer me the one thing I truly want but you make it meaningless. And that, laugh at this one, is the devil's handiwork.

(She exits. He moves downstage. JAKE's apartment door, wooden chair, and mattress are struck. DEBORAH's apartment door is set.)

Scene Four – Outside Deborah's Apartment

JAKE. Me? I come from three generations of depressives. Just part of life like haircuts. But I combine that with unreasoning fear, crippling self-doubt, unmanageable ego, passionate substance abuse, violent tendencies, pleasure from pain and an addiction to In And Out Burgers which is the perfect resume for LA. *(A pause)* Not kidding.

(He walks over and gets into a sleeping bag outside **DEBORAH***'s apartment, she walks out her door dressed for an audition. He sits up just as she turns from locking her door. She lets out an involuntary scream.)*

JAKE. Just me.

DEBORAH. What the hell are you doing?

JAKE. You said 'hell'.

DEBORAH. How did you know where I live?

JAKE. I hired somebody.

DEBORAH. What!

JAKE. Look, could we just go inside for a minute?

DEBORAH. No, we couldn't, you…

JAKE. Listen…

DEBORAH. Did you sleep out here?

JAKE. Not much. I want…

DEBORAH. I have an audition.

JAKE. I want you to audition but…

DEBORAH. Move out of my way.

JAKE. But first I want to apologize.

DEBORAH. For which part of this?

JAKE. For all of it, but particularly for saying 'Fuck'.

*(***DEBORAH***, startled into laughter, puts her head in her hands.)*

And if you will accept my apology, I would be honored if you would audition for Ophelia.

DEBORAH. You would be honored?

JAKE. Yeah.

DEBORAH. You would be honored?

JAKE. Yeah.

DEBORAH. An actual audition?

JAKE. Yeah.

DEBORAH. Where?

JAKE. I don't know. Here.

DEBORAH. In the stairwell?

JAKE. Yeah, or…

(He gestures toward her apartment.)

DEBORAH. We're not going in there.

JAKE. Look, we go into rehearsal in two weeks. There is NO Ophelia. I've seen… two hundred women.

DEBORAH. What's wrong with them?

JAKE. They're disposable. They make Ophelia noises. She can't be disposable to

me. To get out of this alive, I have to believe this stuff.

DEBORAH. And I don't strike you as disposable?

JAKE. No. No you don't.

(A pause. She reaches into her purse.)

DEBORAH. Here's my resume. I don't have an agent so it has my answering service. Have the casting agent call with an appointment. Did people see you out here?

JAKE. A couple.

DEBORAH. *(Pause)* You're in my way, Mr. Abadjian. *(He steps aside.)* I look forward to the audition. But, but do not ever…ever…ever…set foot in my building again. Really.

JAKE. Copasetic.

DEBORAH. Bye.

(She exits. He does the world's tiniest victory dance. She moves downstage. **DEBORAH***'s apartment door is struck.*

JAKE's *apartment door [doubled as audition door], audition table and chair are set.)*

DEBORAH. It took me...a long time...to understand why Christians are mocked and dismissed and even found offensive...and crucified. Particularly Renewalist Christians like myself, which means I have an interactive sense of God's presence. That's right, I talk to God, in a manner of speaking. But let's not go there. And it's fear, this christophobia...for obvious reasons, because if hedonism, and selfrealization and materialism aren't it, then we're talking wasted lives. If there's no Santa Claus there can't be the Christ, right? But there is, he speaks to me. He does.

Scene Five – Audition

(She moves through a door and sees JAKE *sitting at a small table with a single chair.)*

DEBORAH. Hi.

JAKE. Hi.

DEBORAH. The director? The producer?

JAKE. Told them I'd take care of it.

DEBORAH. Please tell me it's not just you seeing me?

JAKE. Yeah, but…

DEBORAH. You can't seem to understand…

JAKE. And you don't understand…

DEBORAH. Wait…

JAKE. What I need.

DEBORAH. I am not here on your behalf, Mr. Abadjian, I am here on my behalf. My family, my friends, my community believe my work is to save souls and that this 'acting' is a corruption of that great purpose but they dare not condemn me because Jesus Christ tells me, no, demands of me, that I do this- and you mock me, sinner.

JAKE. Godamnit! In every audition you have ever done, there is somebody at this table who has the power to hire you. Sometimes they are very, very wise and sometimes they don't know jackshit. This time I am at the table, I have the power, so do your audition or shut up!

(She starts *to go and then circles around and ends up in front of him about eight feet away.)*

DEBORAH. I am Deborah Elling and… *(A pause)* I will be doing Cordelia from Lear.

JAKE. Thank you.

DEBORAH. Oh my dear Father, restoration hang thy medicine on my lips and let the kiss repair those violent harms that my two sisters have in thy reverence made.

Was this a face to be exposed against the warring wind to stand against the deep dread – bolted thunder, in the most terrible and nimble stroke of quick cross lightening to watch with this thin helm? Mine enemy's dog though he had bit me, should have stood that night against my fire. And wast thou fain, poor father, to hovel thee with swine and rogues, forlorn in short and musty straw? Alack, alack, 'tis wonder that thy life and wits at once had not concluded all! He wakes. Speak to him.

(She finishes and stands simply in front of **JAKE**. *He picks up* a *script of Hamlet, opens it at a bookmark and reads almost without emphasis.)*

JAKE. Nymph in thy orisons, be all my sins remembered.

DEBORAH. *(She answers as Ophelia. She knows the scene.)* Good my Lord, How does your honor for this many a day?

JAKE. I humbly thank you, well, well, well.

DEBORAH. My Lord, I have remembrances of yours that I have longed long to redeliver I pray you, now receive them.

JAKE. I Never gave you ought.

DEBORAH. My honored Lord, you know right well you did. And with them words of so sweet breath composed as made the things more rich. Their perfume lost. Take these again.

JAKE. *(He holds up a hand to stop her. A pause. He throws the book at her. She steps back startled.)* Thanks.

(He walks out. She picks up the book and exits. Lights change. **JAKE***'s apartment door, audition table and chair are struck. One chair is set for* **DEBORAH**. **JAKE** *is on one side of the stage,* **DEBORAH** *on the other. He finishes dialing his cell phone. Hers rings. She looks at it and then takes the call.)*

Scene Six – Phone Call

DEBORAH. Hello.

JAKE. Hello.

DEBORAH. Who is this?

JAKE. Jake.

> *(She cuts off the call. He dials back, her phone rings. She cuts it off. He dials back. She answers.)*

DEBORAH. What do you want, Jake?

JAKE. I'm scared.

DEBORAH. I have to protect myself, Jake.

JAKE. Look, I'm a jerk, I behaved like a jerk.

DEBORAH. Yes.

> *(She cuts off the call. He redials. It rings. She doesn't answer. We hear her recorded voice.)*

> *(Recording: You've reached Deborah Elling. Please leave a message.)*

JAKE. *(Leaving the message)* It was so easy for you. How can I...

> *(He cuts off the call. Lights change. The chair is struck.* **DEBORAH** *exits.)*

> *(***JAKE** *moves down and talks to the audience. He's drinking a beer.)*

JAKE. Man that tastes good. I haven't had a beer in eight months. I was a good guy when I drank. I liked everybody... Really. This guy panhandled me in a grocery parking lot. Ex-Serviceman, clean clothes, crutches. I took him to a bank and gave him $8,000 in cash. He hit me up again yesterday, I gave him a dollar. You ever feel like parts of you sloughing off, you know, like paint peeling? It's not good. It's not good.

Scene Seven – Outside Deborah's Apartment

*(He is handed wild flowers. **DEBORAH**'s door is set. He goes and knocks on her door. He knocks again and she enters pulling on a robe over a nightgown.)*

DEBORAH. Who is it?

JAKE. You know who it is.

DEBORAH. It's three o'clock in the morning.

JAKE. You know the only thing I was good at? Cows. I could drive cattle like a son of a bitch...gun.And my Dad, Dad the rancher...I lost six head once...six cows...it's hard to lose cows actually. He told me to undress down to my shorts and then ran me into a barb-wire fence and he never brought it up again. You feel sorry for me?

DEBORAH. Yes.

JAKE. So will you let me in?

DEBORAH. No.

JAKE. You sing?

DEBORAH. Yes. Why?

JAKE. I don't know. When I came back from Pakistan...

DEBORAH. Pakistan?

JAKE. I didn't mean Pakistan...

DEBORAH. You were...

JAKE. Yeah. Yeah. Listen, I have flowers for you out here. You want 'em?

DEBORAH. *(Getting him back on track)* Back from where?

JAKE. Yeah, I was...not well. No job. I started playing some music with these guys...we had a garage band when we were kids. So, uh, we got some gigs and managed a three week tour in California. You play?

DEBORAH. Music wasn't allowed in the house.

JAKE. No music?

DEBORAH. Sacred music. Not a lot of sacred music garage bands.

JAKE. I had a brother and two sisters, everybody played. *(Pause.)* You want a beer?

DEBORAH. I've never had a beer.

JAKE. Are you shitting me? *(No answer.)* Wow. Jesus says no beer?

DEBORAH. Stop.

JAKE. So we did the California dates and at Venice Beach this guy gives me his card and two weeks later I test for Dawnwalker. You see those films?

DEBORAH. I'm sorry, I didn't.

JAKE. He doesn't talk.

DEBORAH. You said.

JAKE. Look, can I come in there and give you these flowers and get you to taste a beer?

DEBORAH. No, you can't.

JAKE. I'm not with anybody. The last woman I was with she…

DEBORAH. I read that, I'm very sorry. She…

JAKE. Now I just fuck people. They come, they go. Look…

DEBORAH. You should go home, Jake, I have to get up early and help my dad.

JAKE. Help him how?

DEBORAH. Get the snakes ready for the service.

JAKE. What?!

DEBORAH. Go on, Jake.

JAKE. I am really sorry about the audition.

DEBORAH. Yeah, well, I was mortified. I cried all the way back on the subway.

JAKE. Yeah. Well how good you were mortified me.

DEBORAH. Jake, you can't…

JAKE. May I please give you these flowers? Please.

DEBORAH. I don't…

JAKE. Just hand them through the door. *(A pause. She opens the door.)* Hey.

DEBORAH. Hey. *(Obviously not store bought.)* Where did you get those?

JAKE. I grabbed a train out of the city and got off where I saw flowers.

DEBORAH. Thank you.

JAKE. I like trains.

DEBORAH. I like flowers.

JAKE. Would you…

DEBORAH. No

JAKE. Let me…

DEBORAH. No to whatever.

JAKE. Have a picnic…

DEBORAH. NO.

JAKE. with me…

DEBORAH. NO.

JAKE. On your stairs.

DEBORAH. *(Laughing in spite of herself)* On the stairs?

JAKE. Yeah, out here…

DEBORAH. Jake…

JAKE. Tomorrow. Twelve o'clock.

DEBORAH. What is this?

JAKE. It's a picnic.

DEBORAH. What-is-this?

JAKE. I like you, shoot me.

DEBORAH. You've been behaving as if you like me?

JAKE. Ummm…maybe not all the time. Please. I would like very much a picnic with you. I have a guy has the best pastrami.

DEBORAH. I don't eat pastrami.

JAKE. You eat what?

DEBORAH. Vegetables.

JAKE. When I was a kid I would scrape the vegetables off my plate, put them in my pocket, and throw them in the incinerator.

DEBORAH. We have our differences.

JAKE. Twelve o'clock on the stairs with vegetables.

(A pause)

DEBORAH. Deal. *(Closes him out. Through door.)* I'm assuming this isn't formal.

JAKE. Fine. Formal.

(He exits. She closes the door and moves down to the audience. Her door is moved upstage and a picnic blanket is set downstage.)

DEBORAH. Men, I think are... drawn to me because I'm... impossible...the sex. I'm twenty-six and I'm...saving myself, which always gets a good laugh; I have a friend who says, 'Careful you'll get stale.' We are sexual beings. I am...profoundly...a sexual being. As are nuns, for instance, they just don't act on it. Christianity is profoundly relational, as sex should be. The gospel is abundant. I want the power of sexuality to find release in Christian marriage. Why am I talking abut this?!

Scene Eight – Picnic on Stairs

(A red checkered table cloth is on the floor. There is a rose in a vase. Both are sitting on floor. **JAKE** *wears a tux shirt, bow tie and suspenders with jeans, carries on picnic food in 2 shopping bags.)*

DEBORAH. May I ask why you live in an apartment with no furniture?

JAKE. Army buddy sublet.

DEBORAH. You could live anywhere.

JAKE. *(Coldly logical)* Do suicides care? *(Change of tone)* We got root vegetables. We got a broccoli, mushroom, onion thing, a salad thing, and a stuffed pepper thing. We got ginger lemonade, vegan chocolate cake and a citrus-pear-pomegranate compote.

DEBORAH. This is…amazing. We can't possibly eat all this.

JAKE. I'll take it to the vegetarian homeless shelter.

DEBORAH. Okay, you're funny.

JAKE. It doesn't help.

DEBORAH. So, you must be in rehearsal?

JAKE. No.

DEBORAH. You're not?

JAKE. It all got delayed.

DEBORAH. No. Why?

JAKE. *(Simply)* Waiting for you.

DEBORAH. That's a joke, right? *(He shakes his head.)* The rehearsal got delayed or the opening got delayed?

JAKE. Both.

(A pause)

DEBORAH. What about the actors?

JAKE. We lost a couple.

DEBORAH. Are you crazy?

JAKE. Yeah.

DEBORAH. You…you can't do that.

JAKE. I can, yeah, because Dawnwalker is an ordinary cabdriver born without a tongue who discovered his superpowers and destroys legions of incubi and succubi from hell running an international monetary scam thus making Dreamworks hundreds of millions of dollars and thus a god who can change at will the opening date of a limited run of Hamlet on Broadway.

DEBORAH. Jake…

JAKE. And just to warn you, I am crazy. My mom said I was crazy, my teachers said I was crazy, Louisa said I was crazy, the army said I was crazy, three psychotherapists said I was crazy and I say I'm crazy. There's an incredible amount of stuff I can't make sense of, myself as one example, so I get drawn to stuff that I instinctually think makes sense even if I can't explain it and the most recent example would be you. Now you should drink your ginger-lemonade before the ice melts. *(She does.)*

Acting, for instance, is senseless. Why? What intrinsic value does it have? For people who watch it, it works in the same way as miniature golf. It's one of a hundred distractions that get us through a meaningless landscape.

DEBORAH. Really?

JAKE. But I recognize Shakespeare is a different deal. He knows something and out of this mysterious knowledge he makes poetry that kills. So I thought I would attach my meaningless self to his meaningful self and see if it worked like a transfusion. *(She starts to speak.)* Wait. But, see, I'm terrified. I read the play and my hands shake. But because I'm crazy, I have this instinct, this blind drive that tells me that the play will clean me like a hot-shower, that I will go out there night after night, consider suicide and reject it as dishonorable, and I have a Jones for honor. *(She starts to speak.)* Wait. But my will is diminished and my fear is great and I need your certainty to get me there. I need somebody with a larger purpose…somebody God speaks to, to put some steel in my shaken self, because I can't do this on my own, surrounded by…Thespians. Please help me.

(A pause.)

DEBORAH. I would like very much to play Ophelia to your Hamlet, Jake.

JAKE. Thank you. Eat.

(The lights change. He exits. She comes downstage. The picnic blanket and **DEBORAH***'s door is struck. An armchair, a Koi pond and a table with two chairs are set.* **DEBORAH** *sits in the armchair.)*

DEBORAH. No, Dad. No, Dad. No. Yes I… like him. No, I don't think he's 'Found.' I'm guessing he hasn't accepted Christ as…what is this? He's the guy playing Hamlet, I play Ophelia, we talk. Talk. I love you but you drive me crazy! Dad… dad… I'm twentysix and I've had way too much practice keeping my legs crossed. *(She laughs.)* Yes, I know God knows what I've been doing and I hope he has some tips for the mad scene. Will you please not worry, please? And that guy you set me up with quoted Corinthians all night. No more dates that are bible study, okay?

(Lights change. **DEBORAH** *and* **JAKE** *are in a Szechuan restaurant. The armchair is struck.)*

Scene Nine – Szechuan Restaurant

DEBORAH. No really, there's a Popeye version of Hamlet. You could do 'Rogue and peasant slave eating spinach.'

JAKE. Can I see you sometime outside a restaurant?

DEBORAH. *(Smiling)* No. Be satisfied it's the best Szechuan on the west side.

JAKE. I sucked today, right?

DEBORAH. You didn't suck.

JAKE. The scansion. The scansion!

DEBORAH. Who cares, you were adorable.

JAKE. What?

DEBORAH. Every actor in that rehearsal wishes they believed every word they said.

JAKE. The Brits hate me. They call me 'The Colonial.' *(An imitation)* "You know dear boy, the scansion gives you the meaning and the interpretation. I'm certainly not saying there's only one way to do it, but we might consider Shakespeare's way, don't you think"

DEBORAH. Okay, agreed, he's a pompous ass, but, hey, he's playing Polonius…problem explained.

JAKE. They pat me. "Good Job, lad." Pat, pat. "Well, we'll give it another go tomorrow, eh?" Pat, pat. Sometimes they just walk by me and pat me.

DEBORAH. Your director called you 'authentic'.

JAKE. Yeah, between dawn and sunrise as long as I don't talk.

DEBORAH. You talk fine.

JAKE. It's fucking hard.

DEBORAH. And?

JAKE. I don't do hard stuff.

DEBORAH. Don't be a baby.

JAKE. Enough. Look, I'm out of rehearsal for two days.

DEBORAH. Your award.

JAKE. Maybe.

DEBORAH. I think that's amazing.

JAKE. Right. It's the fan awards, Deborah, not the Golden Globes, all right?

DEBORAH. Chosen by millions of people.

JAKE. Yeah, Dawnwalker changed their lives.

DEBORAH. Cheap to be snide.

JAKE. Point taken. Listen…

DEBORAH. *(Looking at watch)* Shoot, I have to…

(She starts to get up.)

JAKE. So getting baptized means what?

DEBORAH. *(Stops. Suspicious)* Your admission into the community of Christians.

JAKE. And this happened when you were six?

DEBORAH. You just have to be old enough to be instructed in the gospel.

JAKE. And then I'm saved, right?

DEBORAH. Without baptism you cannot enter heaven. Baptism is rebirth.

JAKE. Okay.

DEBORAH. And it symbolizes repentance. Have you been baptized?

JAKE. Not while I was awake. A ticket to heaven, I could use that though.

DEBORAH. And repentance?

JAKE. I've got plenty to repent.

DEBORAH. I could baptize you.

JAKE. Don't you have to be clergy?

DEBORAH. Not in an emergency.

JAKE. And I'm an emergency?

DEBORAH. You are definitely an emergency.

JAKE. Thanks.

DEBORAH. I could do it here.

JAKE. In a Szechuan restaurant?

DEBORAH. There's the pool with the Koi in it.

JAKE. Yeah, right. Is there such a thing as Szechuan dessert?

DEBORAH. I dare you.

JAKE. *(Pause)* You dare me? You shouldn't dare me, lady.

DEBORAH. Well, if you don't have the *cojones*.

JAKE. Whoa, listen to you! You got to put my head under water?

DEBORAH. Immersion, right. Yes or no?

JAKE. This is a good suit.

DEBORAH. I dare you, pussy.

JAKE. Let's go.

> *(He crosses to Koi pool.)*

DEBORAH. Do you renounce Satan and evil?

JAKE. For the evening.

DEBORAH. Hands. *(They take hands.)* Do you accept Jesus Christ as your Lord and Savior?

JAKE. You notice everybody has stopped eating?

DEBORAH. Do you accept Jesus Christ as your Lord and Savior?

JAKE. I'll say I do.

DEBORAH. Kneel down. *(He shakes his head.)* Chicken. *(He stares at her, then kneels. She grabs his hair:* **JAKE:** *Ow!)* Then in obedience to our Lord and Savior, Jesus Christ… *(Takes him firmly by the hair.)* And your profession of Faith… *(Pushes him underwater.)* I baptize you, Jake Robert Abajian, in the name of the Father, Son and Holy Spirit, Amen.

> *(She lets him up, gasping for air and soaked. We hear applause and Chinese delight from the other diners.)*

JAKE. *(To the crowd)* Thank you, thank you very much. *(***DEBORAH*** starts laughing.)* So, my dominant, am I saved now?

DEBORAH. No.

JAKE. What?

DEBORAH. You were coerced. Doesn't count.

(She starts to go.)

JAKE. Go with me.

DEBORAH. Where?

JAKE. To the awards.

DEBORAH. *(Staring at the ground)* Jake.

JAKE. Have some fun for one day in your miserable life.

DEBORAH. I don't have a miserable life.

JAKE. Fine. Have some fun for one day in my miserable life.

DEBORAH. This is like the definition of a bad idea.

JAKE. Okay, you have to listen...

DEBORAH. I can't.

JAKE. For one minute. I have to be able to do this play. Imperative. Have to. The scene that sets the table for me is your Ophelia scene when she give him back his gifts. It turns him. She's the only emotional center he ever had. Wait. Wait. We agreed they've slept together and...

DEBORAH. I have a commercial audition in...

JAKE. But that's not real in the scene. You said it was somehow sanitized and you're right. We're, I don't know, skating on the surface so we need to go there, take that chance. Go with me to L.A., because it's really, really clear we can't open up the scene until we have the courage to fuck.

DEBORAH. Wow. That is unbelievably creepy and... *(He breaks up laughing.)* What are you laughing at?

JAKE. Joking! I was joking. Oh my God, you should have seen your face.

DEBORAH. You think that was funny?

JAKE. *(Throwing his hands up in the air in exasperation)* Deborah! Come to LA, wear a great dress, dance with me at the after party, drink ginger ale and bunk with my mom.

DEBORAH. Your mom?

JAKE. Yeah, my mom. She wants to see me get an award and she's afraid to sleep in a hotel by herself. Please. This stuff terrifies me and it terrifies her. You are allowed to dance, right?

DEBORAH. Yes, I'm allowed to dance.

JAKE. Look, if I'm too dangerous we can fly on separate planes.

DEBORAH. Jake, you are…clumsy. You have no idea what to do with a woman except sleep with her.

JAKE. So far.

DEBORAH. Your mom knows who I am?

JAKE. Yeah.

DEBORAH. Who does she think I am?

JAKE. I'm not answering that.

DEBORAH. Will I meet movie stars?

JAKE. Everybody you ever saw in a movie.

DEBORAH. Rudolph Valentino?

JAKE. In this century.

DEBORAH. May I bring my father?

JAKE. He knows who I am?

DEBORAH. He does, yes.

JAKE. Who does he think I am?

DEBORAH. He thinks you play Hamlet.

JAKE. Bring your whole family only you have to share with my mom.

DEBORAH. *(A pause)* I can't afford it.

JAKE. Deborah.

DEBORAH. What?

JAKE. Let *me* do this.

DEBORAH. No.

JAKE. How many times a day do you say 'No.'

DEBORAH. As many as I have to.

JAKE. What the hell am I supposed to do with the money? You can't get rid of that shit! Would you mind if I got like this much pleasure? Oh, Oh, I said 'pleasure,'

I must have scared your constricted pretzel of a protestant soul to death! Deborah, Deborah, you would do me a terrific favor if you went to LA on my dime. You and your snake handling father.

DEBORAH. He doesn't really handle snakes.

JAKE. What?

DEBORAH. That was a joke.

JAKE. You are a weird chick.

DEBORAH. *(Pleased)* Really?

JAKE. Yes, really.

DEBORAH. But I would owe you and eventually you would want to collect. That's how it works.

JAKE. That's how it works if you're a clinical paranoid. Go to LA. The networking is like no networking you have ever heard of. You are beautiful and talented and unbelievably strange. They love that! And I have to buy you a dress because you dress for shit. Who's your favorite movie star?

DEBORAH. Ralph Fiennes

JAKE. He will hit on you like a drum. I will have to pry him off with the Jaws-of-Life.

DEBORAH. *(Laughing)* Really?

JAKE. But my mom won't let Ralph in the room because she sleeps in thermal underwear which tends to put off men.

DEBORAH. And I sleep in my fathers pajamas.

JAKE. Don't turn me on. Deborah, listen. No, look at me. I am asking you humbly to do this, as a Christian Martyr. I behave badly in public and need to be restrained. Look at me. This is your airline ticket, it's first class. Flight 1470 out of La Guardia, ten-forty tomorrow. I'm going tonight because of interviews and the fact that you think sitting next to me on a plane might make you pregnant.

DEBORAH. Jake...

JAKE. My mom will meet you at LAX with a limo. Here's
    her cell. You will recognize her because she looks like
    a delighted toad.

DEBORAH. Jake…

JAKE. Ball in your court. Figure it out.

*(He exits. She stands. Lights change. The stage is struck.
DEBORAH is dressed for the awards while she talks to the
audience.)*

DEBORAH. The ontological argument, not to believe in
    God, is irrational. See Descartes. Once you mentally
    grasp God as a concept, we see his non-existence is
    impossible. The universe came into existence. Nothing
    comes into existence unless something brings it into
    existence. Nothing comes from nothing. That which
    brought the universe into existence could not fail
    to exist. That's a little mixed up with the first cause
    argument but sue me. The teleological argument: this
    is an argument that tries to prove the existence of
    God from the fact the universe is ordered. Universes
    we know have not allowed for the existence of life.
    That ours does implies that the existence of a creator
    who has designed it with humanity in mind. The
    moral argument: If we look at the authoritative nature
    of morality. It transcends all human authority and
    thus must have been commanded by a being whose
    authority transcends human authority.

(She is dressed for the awards.)

Finally, God and only God could make me look this
good.

Scene Ten – Award Ceremony

DEBORAH. Wow. You can dance.

JAKE. My mom ran cotillion for seventeen years.

DEBORAH. *(Looking around)* Is that?

JAKE. Anne Hathaway.

DEBORAH. And that's…

JAKE. Ethan Hawke.

DEBORAH. This is like the mad-hatters tea party. *(They dance.)* You're quiet. Is it painful you didn't win?

JAKE. It's painful not to care.

DEBORAH. Are you sure you don't care?

JAKE. I'm just some guy who wandered in and was mistaken for an actor.

DEBORAH. You're so cruel to yourself.

JAKE. Feels right.

DEBORAH. I see the actor you are. It's painfully honest.

JAKE. I don't like compliments, all right? I don't want to hear it.

DEBORAH. What is it you do want to hear?

JAKE. Don't patronize me.

(They stop dancing. The music continues.)

DEBORAH. These are accomplished, powerful people. They come over to include you and you freeze them like an ice storm. Would it kill you to be gracious? It isn't everybody's fault that you don't like yourself very much.

JAKE. And you, do you like me?

DEBORAH. Obviously.

JAKE. Let's go outside, I can't do this.

(He leaves her. She stands for a moment and then follows him. The music becomes fainter. They are 'outside'.)

DEBORAH. No Ralph Fiennes

JAKE. No, I made that up. You want a cigarette?

DEBORAH. I…

JAKE. Right, you never had a cigarette or anal sex.

DEBORAH. You don't shock me.

JAKE. You don't know enough to be shocked, Deborah.

    (A pause)

DEBORAH. Did you see your mom dancing with Christopher
    Plummer?

JAKE. (A sudden laugh) And I guarantee you, she has no
    idea who he is.

DEBORAH. That probably turns him on.

JAKE. Believe me, that doesn't turn him on.

    (She laughs.)

    Smoke a blunt with me?

    (She shakes her head.)

    Strip naked and dance for me.

DEBORAH. Not right now, but thanks for asking. Oh, Jake.

JAKE. What is it exactly that Jesus does for you?

DEBORAH. Is that an ironic question or a real question?

JAKE. That, Deborah, is a real fucking question.

DEBORAH. Makes sense out of chaos.

JAKE. What if its just chaos?

DEBORAH. Same difference, Jake. "I have come as a light
    into the world, that everyone who believes in me may
    not remain in the darkness."

JAKE. Fine. I get it.

DEBORAH. I feel the light, Jake. Right now. My father lives
    only to bring others to the path, but I'm not called to
    do that.

JAKE. Yeah, he's in there now bringing the light to the
    biggest dominatrix in Hollywood. And please, don't
    say what's a 'dominatrix.'

DEBORAH. Plays dominoes?

JAKE. Very funny.

DEBORAH. I have a call to serve… Well, actually share. I try to share the beautiful and true…don't make a face… and when I can do that, Jake, I feel the good.

(A pause)

So, is this the right small talk for this occasion?

JAKE. I think it has nothing to do with anything I can understand.

DEBORAH. And my father would say that's the darkness

JAKE. Okay…

DEBORAH. and the darkness is the pain…

JAKE. Okay…

DEBORAH. and the pain is the absence of light.

JAKE. It's maybe not the right moment to convert me, Deborah.

DEBORAH. I wouldn't have the strength. But you know what I would like very, very much?

JAKE. I can't imagine.

DEBORAH. I would like you to take me back to Fantasyland and hold me in your arms and dance with me just as close to Vigo Mortensen as we can get.

JAKE. Hey, that would be my dream too.

(She steps into his arms and they waltz like demons to the edge of the stage where he releases her, she exits, and he moves upstage. As he talks he changes, with assistance into jeans and a t-shirt. A bar table, two bar stools, empty whiskey bottle and shot glass are set down stage.)

I can't do this part. Who can do this part? It makes no sense! He won't kill Claudius… who has murdered his father by the way…because of his religion we gather, but he has to kill him because of his honor, so he agonizes, he agonizes, he agonizes and kills Polonius, which is okay for some reason, flees to England, jumps ship and ends up with pirates, how am I suppose to act pirates, makes it back to Ophelia's funeral, who he drove to suicide, and is, we don't know why, an entirely different guy. Now he wants to kill everybody. Jumps into Ophelia's grave and punches out her brother. What, we might ask, is going on here? He leaves out all the key scenes from 'can't Kill Claudius' to 'Must Kill Claudius' and what the hell kind of writing is that? This is the greatest play ever written? This is the guy who brought psychology to the stage? It's a con game of a play by a playwright who very possibly didn't write it, done for an elderly audience who use it to punish their grandchildren, by snobbish British actors who despise the audience and think an emotion is when you take your voice down half an octave, for critics who invariably say you aren't as good as the guy who played it last year, and because the playwright, having no idea how to end it, just kills everybody! And what is worst of all, insufferable, is that everybody has advice. Everybody. What the hell was I thinking?! What? Bartender, another bottle and a clean glass. Yeah, I was on the floor but I got up.

Scene Eleven – Bar

*(**DEBORAH** enters.)*

DEBORAH. Jake.

(He turns.)

JAKE. Oh look, it's Salvation Nell. Well, you look hot. Which one of the commandments do you represent?

DEBORAH. You missed rehearsal.

JAKE. Well, that's just totally fucking irresponsible.

(She slaps him hard.)

Yeah, well.

DEBORAH. Who do you think you are, Jake?

JAKE. Good fucking question.

DEBORAH. We sat there, eighteen people, for two hours and they didn't want to release us in case our movie star deigned to show up.

JAKE. Blah Blah Blah…

DEBORAH. The stage manager wanted to call the police but I talked her out of that.

JAKE. Thanks for having my interests at heart.

DEBORAH. Actually I had my interests at heart. Do you understand there are other people in the world? We have three days until we tech and you haven't even bothered to learn the lines from Act V on?

JAKE. Yeah, well, wherever I've gone and whatever I've done, there's always been someone like you keeping score. Sit the hell down, have a drink, and tell me what's wrong with me.

DEBORAH. You're an asshole.

JAKE. Bingo!

DEBORAH. And if you screw this up, walk out on it or just blow it off, that just makes you colorful, sells a lot of supermarket magazines and ups your price per picture. But the rest of us, the ones with the unimportant lives,

who took a ride on your coattails hoping a little shine
would rub off on us and we could have a tiny slice of
your monumental pie, we're just supposed to chalk
this up to 'droit du signeur,' is that it?

JAKE. What?

DEBORAH. That's the legal right of the lord of a medieval
estate to take the virginity of his serf's maiden
daughters.

JAKE. Sounds like how it works. Sorry I don't take dress up
as divine service. And, by the way, what makes your
virginity, which somehow I forget taking, so valuable
in this whorehouse? Oh, I forgot, Jesus is supposed to
get it.

(She slaps him again.)

You know someday, you arrogant little twat, you're
going to get the hell kicked out of you and it will be
richly deserved. And by the way, everybody in that
rehearsal room took the job on the basis of my coattails
and knew I was an asshole, so they can't play horrified
now.

DEBORAH. I'm not naive, Jake, I've even flirted with you a
little bit to make this work but...

JAKE. I noticed. I actually never met a woman who doesn't
flirt with me because I have a target on my chest. Now.
This is a drink. There, drink it. Otherwise get out.

DEBORAH. Self-loathing is cheap and lazy.

JAKE. What are you doing?

DEBORAH. I'm calling stage management to let them know
you're alive.

JAKE. Are you in love with me?

DEBORAH. *(On the phone)* Shut up, Jake.

JAKE. Did you know that a list of books about Hamlet would
be longer than the Toledo phone book?

DEBORAH. *(Off the phone)* Listen to me!

JAKE. Squids have three hearts.

DEBORAH. Listen to me!

JAKE. Your ears are actually gigantic.

DEBORAH. I'm taking you to my apartment.

JAKE. Apartment?

DEBORAH. Where I am going to feed and coffee you, put you to bed, lock you in and then go sleep at my sisters.

JAKE. What will you feed me?

DEBORAH. Tomorrow I will wake you up, force you to shower, eat breakfast and learn the lines from Act V and make sure you're at the one o'clock rehearsal. None of this...listen to me...is for your benefit and you are going to do this because you owe me. You owe me!

JAKE. In an ordered universe, right?

DEBORAH. Now get up.

JAKE. Tell me you love me.

DEBORAH. I don't love you, Jake.

JAKE. You sure?

DEBORAH. I have a cab outside. Walk.

JAKE. Do you think I love you?

DEBORAH. Love won't help you, Jake.

JAKE. Can Jesus help me?

DEBORAH. Yes, Jesus can help you.

JAKE. If he was fucking real.

DEBORAH. And try not to blaspheme. It's not that hard.

(He staggers. She supports him.)

Walk.

*(They exit. Bar table and chairs struck. **DEBORAH**'s door, a sofa, coffee table and kitty dish, is placed to represent her apartment. She moves him to it.)*

Scene Twelve – Deborah's Apartment

DEBORAH. Now sit.

(He sits.)

JAKE. *(Looking around him)* Wow. Biblical lunatics are really neat.

DEBORAH. *(Chuckling)* You are impossible.

JAKE. My most attractive feature.

DEBORAH. We're not going into that.

(She hands him a plate.)

JAKE. What's this?

DEBORAH. They call this pie, Jake.

JAKE. What kind of pie?

DEBORAH. Heirloom apple pie.

JAKE. You made this?

DEBORAH. I did, yes.

JAKE. I'm being served Heirloom apple pie by a demented virgin who baptized me in a Szechuan restaurant.

DEBORAH. Pretty cool, huh?

JAKE. *(Taking a chain off his neck with his dog tags and a key on it)* Take this.

DEBORAH. What is it?

JAKE. Those are dog tags so the army knows who you are after they kill you.

DEBORAH. And the key?

JAKE. To my apartment.

DEBORAH. Why?

JAKE. You might need it.

DEBORAH. Why?

JAKE. Because it would improve my mood to mistakenly believe you might visit me.

DEBORAH. Well…

JAKE. Do you ever get depressed?

DEBORAH. Yes.

JAKE. Really depressed?

DEBORAH. Yes.

JAKE. You plan to say more than yes?

DEBORAH. No.

JAKE. I grew up in a singlewide 1975 Tomboy trailer…kitty, kitty…that was such a mess I never saw the floor. There were, however, five hundred salt & pepper shakers in the shape of pigs. And my father beat me with a length of trailer chain and cut my mother in her sleep.

DEBORAH. Jake!

JAKE. Well, actually he didn't but it would explain me right? *(Pause)* Any more pie?

DEBORAH. I'll bring another slice.

JAKE. Just bring me the pie. *(She exits and returns shortly with the pie.)* My father was part of a crew handling the Krupp-Bagger 288 which was, at that time, the world's largest trencher. It was like this 13,500-ton mobile strip miner…

DEBORAH. Wow.

JAKE. and he traveled all over the country with this thing…

DEBORAH. That's unbelievable…

JAKE. …and we hardly ever saw him. When he was home he sat in a recliner in the yard and read Louis L'Amour novels 'til he left when I was sixteen and good riddance. Yours?

DEBORAH. He did real estate. He got the call while he was showing a condo.

JAKE. Of course he did.

DEBORAH. Jake…

JAKE. Why?

DEBORAH. Because he needed it.

JAKE. Jesus personally spoke to him?

DEBORAH. He did.

JAKE. Saying?

DEBORAH. He said, "Now". *(A pause)*

JAKE. How did he know it was Jesus?

DEBORAH. Don't patronize me. He left his job and founded The Covenant of Christ Alive in an old shoe store.

JAKE. Right. Deborah, look straight at me and tell me Jesus talks to you?

DEBORAH. He does.

JAKE. Like this. Like I am?

DEBORAH. I sense a presence and a meaning.

JAKE. But does he talk to you!? Does he have a voice?

DEBORAH. He has a meaning.

JAKE. I asked you…this is… How is it possible you believe this bullshit?

DEBORAH. Because I hear him with an obedient heart…

JAKE. Forget it.

DEBORAH. And then it is a Joy to serve and a Joy to be.

JAKE. Forget it!

DEBORAH. And that Joy makes all this make sense.

JAKE. Have you got alcohol? Cough medicine?

DEBORAH. Does you life make sense to you?

JAKE. Obviously not.

DEBORAH. So…

JAKE. But I would rather be a true chaos than a false order.

DEBORAH. And I would rather live a false order…

JAKE. How can you…

DEBORAH. If it came to that. Whatever truth you work with makes you miserable.

JAKE. Maybe that's the price of rationality.

DEBORAH. Then the price is too high. I'm going to my sisters.

JAKE. Okay, run chicken shit.

DEBORAH. Sleep. I'll see you in the morning.

JAKE. Deborah.

(She turns and he kisses her. He doesn't force her but he kisses her. She stays in the kiss for a moment then backs away a step.)

No way, huh?

(She steps back in and kisses him hard. Then she turns and goes to the door.)

Okay, marry me.

DEBORAH. That's cruel.

JAKE. Come make breakfast tomorrow morning and then we'll go down to city hall and do it.

DEBORAH. I apologize for kissing you, Jake. I told myself all along I would never do that. You deserve to be angry it was…not kind. It did feel specific though…the kiss… not as if I was just…

JAKE. Another fuck.

DEBORAH. No, it didn't feel like that. But you are way, way, way too much for me. Way too much. You think you are the…shattered vessel and I'm…but you don't know…you have no sense of…the edge I live on. It's razor thin: trust me…so…I… very much appreciate the proposal but I can't marry you.!

JAKE. Because you're better, right? *(She doesn't offer.)* You're humble and gentle but down there where it counts your better.

DEBORAH. I have never thought that.

JAKE. No, you don't think it, you know it. 'Cause you got Jiminy Cricket whispering in your ear.

DEBORAH. You don't know me, Jake.

JAKE. Do I not? I'm around people getting off on feeling better than me all the fucking time. I'm the world champion expert, baby. When we're rehearsing the Tragical Historie of Hamlet with our all-toff supporting cast it's a killing field of feeling better than me. You could cut the smug self-satisfaction with a blunt object.

And you, my little Christlet, play a little double game.
You support me and build me up so it's even spicier
to be better than me… dare I say, more Christian. But
hear me in your obedient heart… you are never going
to meet anyone who needs you more than I do, who is
more amazed by you, more deeply struck, more aware
of your struggle and if you haven't been lying to me
this whole fucking time I ask you to cleave to me and
save my fucking soul.

DEBORAH. I can't. Good night, Jake.

*(She turns to open the door and he grabs her from behind
and turns her into a rough kiss. She fights her way out.
He tries to pull her in and she elbows him in the face.
He picks her up and throws her on the sofa. She tries to
grab the fork on the coffee table, he stops her. She kicks
him back and grabs the fork. He jumps on top of her
knocking the fork out of her hand, they pause. He is on
top of her, pinning her between his legs, about to undo
his pants.)*

Don't…rape me, Jake.

(He freezes.)

Don't.

(He scrambles off her as if scalded.)

JAKE. Shit. Shit! *(He hits the sofa.)* I didn't… I would never…
Oh Christ, your eye I…I swear to you…let me get a
towel and some ice. *(Banging his head on the floor)* Fuck
me. Fuck me!

DEBORAH. Stop it! *(He does.)* Listen to me.

JAKE. I'm garbage…

DEBORAH. Listen to me. *(She is remarkably calm.)* I'm all
right!

JAKE. *(Simultaneously)* Don't tell me you're alright. *(Speaking
alone)*

DEBORAH. Shhhh. Shhh. I'm fine.

JAKE. I would never hurt you.

DEBORAH. Listen to me. You have to go now.

JAKE. Just let me…

DEBORAH. I want you to go, Jake.

JAKE. No, I will.

DEBORAH. And listen to me. If you hurt yourself, try to punish yourself that's the worst kind of cowardice, worse than this Jake, do you understand that?

JAKE. I never intended…

DEBORAH. Get out! Go, Jake.

> (**DEBORAH** *stands shakily then rips off the dog tags and throws them on the couch. She covers her face with her hands.*)

Oh dear God. I'm all right.

(She looks up and breathes.)

I'm alright. I'm alright.

(Walks down stage and dials on her cell phone. The sofa, coffee table, and door are struck leaving a blank stage.)

Scene Thirteen – Prayer/Phone Call

DEBORAH. Dad? I know. I'm sorry... No, I'm alright, I just... I'm not crying... shouldn't have called. I just had a problem with a guy... No, no...just a tussle... Dad, no, don't get on a plane. Nothing happened, nothing. I was just...scared. Please don't. I just needed to...hear your voice. I'm alone, locked in, I'm fine. Dad, you're a Christian not a Sicilian. *(She laughs.)* He won't. No, he won't. Go back to sleep. I'll call in the morning. I promise. God's love, Dad. I'm fine.

(She clicks off. She and JAKE kneel on opposite sides of the stage. Spoken simultaneously.)

DEBORAH. 'I called out to the Lord, out of my distress, and he answered me; out of the belly of Shed I cried, and you heard my voice.'

JAKE. You uh...you have to help me, alright? If you are... all-seeing, you can see I need the help.

DEBORAH. 'For you cast me into the deep, into the heart of the sea's and the flood surrounds me.'

JAKE. If there is a Jesus Christ then I ask him to take me in and make me whole because... I am in pieces and I have done harm. *(Pause)* Nobody home, huh?

DEBORAH. But I with the voice of thanksgiving will sacrifice to you; what I have vowed, I will pay.

JAKE. No organizing principle. What a surprise.

DEBORAH. Give me, oh Lord, the healing power to forgive.

JAKE. How many times do I have to prove I'm a piece of shit before I believe it?

(He exits.)

(She dials JAKE's cell phone. He answers but does not speak.)

DEBORAH. Jake? *(He doesn't answer.)* Jake? Are you alright?

JAKE. Yeah. Great.

DEBORAH. What are you doing?

JAKE. Loathing myself. You?

DEBORAH. I ran into a doorknob.

JAKE. How bad is it?

DEBORAH. Enough to be embarrassed about.

(A pause)

JAKE. I have no idea what to say about this.

DEBORAH. Say it's unforgivable.

JAKE. It's unforgivable.

DEBORAH. Wrong. You've been forgiven.

JAKE. Oh my God.

DEBORAH. You're welcome. You ever, ever do that again Jake, I'll have you arrested, and then I will sue you and have the devil rend your soul and feed it to the hawks. *(Pause)* Are you there?

JAKE. Yeah.

DEBORAH. And thank you for the proposal of marriage. *(Silence)* I do…care for you. But I think we both know what a catastrophe…that would be.

JAKE. Word.

DEBORAH. Should I pick you up on the way to rehearsal?

JAKE. No need.

DEBORAH. You'll be there?

JAKE. Yeah.

DEBORAH. You're sure.

JAKE. I'm sure.

(They both click off. DEBORAH moves downstage. A crew member paints bruises as she talks.)

DEBORAH. "Then Peter came to Jesus and asked 'Lord, how many times shall I forgive my brother when he sins against me? Up to seven times?' Jesus answered, ' I tell you, not seven times but seventy seven times.' Judge not, lest ye be judged. But you will still be incredibly pissed off.

(She exits. Lights change. They both enter empty rehearsal space. They speak to an imaginary cast.)

Scene Fourteen – Rehearsal

DEBORAH. What? I know. I know. No, I'd prefer just to rehearse if you don't mind.

(The voices of the people they talk to are unheard.)

No, I'd like to rehearse... What happened has been taken care of... It looks worse than it is. That wasn't necessary. I don't think...

JAKE. I did. *(A pause.)* I don't deserve to be in the room.

DEBORAH. Jake.

JAKE. There's a lot of places I don't deserve to be.

DEBORAH. Just rehearse.

JAKE. *(With Cockney accent)* It would be amusing to see you try...

(Pause. Tosses script offstage.)

Here. You play it. You've got the accent.

*(He exits. **DEBORAH** follows. They are on the street. A NYC garbage can is set downstage.)*

Scene Fifteen – The Street

DEBORAH. Jake! Jake! Please don't do this.

JAKE. It's done.

DEBORAH. People need the job Jake, and they have the job because you're Dawnwalker. Yes, three of the stupidest movies ever made. But now they get to do Hamlet, and I get to do Hamlet, and you get to do Hamlet. And my mother is coming who has never seen a play, Jake, and I'm going to get a career out of this, and I badly want that, okay? I talk to Jesus, remember, and he wants me to have a career.

(Despite himself, **JAKE** *smiles.)*

And you hate yourself, right? Well this is perfect. Everybody in rehearsal hates you so you've got backup. You know what's right. Do what's right.

*(***JAKE*** exits. Lights change. 2 crew assist her into her Ophelia costume and wipe off bruises. Trash can is struck.)*

Susan May Fort, a former actress who had gone mad after her lovers betrayal, escaped from her keeper, broke into the theatre and just as the Ophelia of the evening was beginning her mad scene, knocked her to the ground and observers said "she was in truth, Ophelia herself." So lets keep the doors locked, okay?

Scene Sixteen – The Dressing Room

(A dressing room table and two chairs are set up.)

DEBORAH. Rosemary, pansies, fennel, columbines, rue… and then what? Daisies? No, herb-grace, then daisies, then violets. Okay, I'm scared now. Relax Deborah, you're a virgin and I doubt a virgin has ever played this role in New York. They won't have a thing to compare you with.

(Sits at dressing table. She does a tongue twister.)

Toy boat, toy boat, toy boat, toy boat, toy boat.

(There's a knock on the dressing room door. **JAKE** *enters as Hamlet.)*

Come.

(She turns.)

Jake, you look fantastic. We're really going to do this, huh? I never really knew what thrilled meant. This is me thrilled.

JAKE. You look thrilled.

DEBORAH. I'm so proud to do this with you. I can't believe anyone has ever been as simple and painful and heartbreaking.

JAKE. Thanks.

DEBORAH. *(Handing him a small packet)* Happy Opening. *(He opens it.)* It's all the great actors who have played Hamlet made up as post cards. Olivier, Burbage, Betterton, Booth…Twenty-three of them. Look at the last one. *(He does.)* See, you.

JAKE. Listen, you have not, in six weeks accepted so much as a cup of coffee from me. We have even gone Dutch on the subway, Deborah. But I would never, never have gotten to this opening night, and I mean alive without your support and forbearance and…forgiveness and… seen through your eyes there is a me I can bear. So I would like you to grit your teeth, show some good manners and accept an opening night present as if you had been well brought up and generous of spirit.

DEBORAH. *(Exhaling)* I will try. You're scaring me again.

(He hands her a present. It's a jewelry box. She opens it.)

DEBORAH. Oh, Jake.

JAKE. It's seventeenth century. Called a Carcanet. Kind of a Tudor choker worn by ladies of high birth.

DEBORAH. Oh, Jake.

JAKE. Supposedly from the decade he wrote Hamlet – give or take twenty years.

DEBORAH. Where on earth could you possibly get this?

JAKE. You'd have to be a superhero.

DEBORAH. This is impossibly beautiful. This is the present of presents. *(A pause)* I know that you...love me, Jake and that...that is...incredibly meaningful to me. I think about it more than...you would imagine and I am...infatuated with what I think you feel...who on earth wouldn't be but...you are too dangerous for me, Jake. And because you are dangerous to my eternal soul...ridiculous as I know you think that is...

(Pause)

I am not free to love you and accept this beautiful gift.

JAKE. Please.

DEBORAH. I can't.

JAKE. Please take this.

DEBORAH. This isn't what tonight is about.

JAKE. Take the goddamned necklace.

DEBORAH. *(Turning away)* We go on in a half hour, Jake.

JAKE. You know what I don't like about "The Good," Deborah, the people who represent "The Good" the people who sail under the banner of "The Good"? They live in little, fenced in minds with well guarded gates, completely ignoring the shit and muck and desperation and battered hopes all around them that needs their fucking attention and usually, and this is the worst part, they aren't very bright which kind of compromises their deal, because "The Good" turned stupid is moral blindness, Deborah, distilled right down to a smug self satisfaction and arrogance which just provokes the shit out of the multitudes crying out for some kind of fucking salvation which you seem unable to even recognize!

(He sweeps everything off her dressing table.)

You're not going to find anybody who loves you Deborah, because you're fucking terrified to get your heart dirty. *(as he exits)* Keep the necklace, give it to the poor.

(The stage is cleared of furniture and strewn props as she exits. We hear, "Places please, Ladies and Gentlemen, for the top of Act One. Places please. Act One places, please." A bare stage. A moment. HAMLET enters from one side, OPHELIA from the other. She is wearing the necklace.)

Scene Seventeen – Onstage

HAMLET. Soft you now, the Fair Ophelia! Nymph in thy orisons be all my sins remembered.

OPHELIA. Good my Lord, how does your honor for this many a day?

HAMLET. I humbly thank you. Well, well, well.

OPHELIA. My Lord, I have remembrances of yours that I have longed long to redeliver. I pray you now, receive them.

HAMLET. No, not I, I never gave you ought.

OPHELIA. My honored Lord, you know right well you did. And with them words of so sweet breath composed As made the things more rich.

(She takes off the necklace.)

Their perfume lost, take these again.

For to the noble mind rich gifts wax poor,

When givers prove unkind.

(She holds the necklace out to him.)

There my Lord.

(He stares at her. He does not take the necklace. Then he laughs and kisses DEBORAH *on the forehead.)*

JAKE. Nice. *(walks far away from her)*

OPHELIA. Lord Hamlet? Lord Hamlet?

HAMLET. Are you honest? Are you fair?

OPHELIA. What means your lordship?

JAKE. That if you be honest and…

(He walks down to the audience and address them. DEBORAH *stays upstage.)*

JAKE. Ladies and gentlemen, my name is Jake Abadjian and Ophelia over there just reminded me I can't give you what you've paid for. Unless, of course, you're in a satirical mood because you have seen or heard of the films where I appear... Thus you would be here to laugh which would be understandable under the circumstances. But I am here for a different reason which... I hoped I was in here somewhere...that I could find myself in this...that I would show up. But i'm not in here... I'm not in here, so I won't burden you with the attempt because I'm...not very good am I? Not much goodness. I can't help you motherfuckers pass the time. Your money will be returned.

(He exits. **DEBORAH** *stands alone.)*

DEBORAH. Just undress me.

(A young woman enters to her. As she is undressed and redressed in street clothes she prays.)

Father, I take a stand, in Jesus name against the darkness. I ask for your protection, that I be signed with the cross of Jesus, sealed with the blood of Jesus, hidden in Christ and protected by your teachings. Protect me, Jesus, from all fascination with sin or evil and may my eyes be open to the beauty, grace and truth of God. Your word is powerful Lord, and accomplishes your purposes. Amen.

(Dressed, she moves off. A large NYC trash can is placed down stage, **JAKE** *enters. He carries a bottle of bourbon.* **DEBORAH** *calls.)*

Scene Eighteen – The Street

DEBORAH. Jake.

(He stops for a second, then turns and continues walking.)

JAKE.

(He stops and turns. She enters, furiously.)

How dare you!

(She pushes him.)

How dare you do that to me!

(She pushes him hard.)

We're all laughing stocks, do you understand? And you left me there!

(She pushes him hard off balance.)

My family was out there, Jake. My high school English teacher was out there. I'm standing there. Standing there! In front of the most powerful critics in the English speaking world! And after years, years of getting to that moment, and I worked to get there Jake, I worked, I'm the stupid little girl Jake Abadjian kissed on the forehead and walked out of the scene. Forever. That's who I am. And day after day after day in rehearsal you said "it's not there, it's not real, it's not happening, there's nothing alive." So I wore the choker so that would happen for you, Jake. I wanted it to happen for you, no matter what you said to me in the dressing room. So now you've raped me publicly and privately, and you know you have, because you are enraged, enraged you are alive and you want everybody, everybody to suffer for it. And you dare, you dare to talk to me about love? I'm afraid to get dirty? I suffer from moral blindness? You are a sick ticket, Jake, you are the plague bearer, and if there is such a thing as evil, you're as close as I'll ever get to it. God forgive you!

*(She exits. He stands looking after her and calmly
uncaps the bottle, drinks and tosses the bottle offstage.
We hear it break. He exits.* **DEBORAH** *re-enters talking
into her cell phone. The trashcan is struck.)*

Scene Nineteen – Jake's apartment

Jake? Jake?

(She punches off and dials again.)

Jake, it's Deborah. Answer the phone, Jake. Answer the phone, Jake. Answer the phone, Jake.

(She punches off and dials again.)

Answer the phone, Jake. Answer the phone, Jake. Answer the phone, Jake. Answer the phone, Jake. I don't deserve this. Please answer the phone.

(She punches off and dials.)

It's Deborah. Please call me, you're scaring me. I need you to call me, Jake. Now. Call me now.

(She waits. No call. She fishes in her bag and pulls out the key to JAKE's apartment on the chain that contains his dog tags. A door is rolled on. She unlocks it with his key. She enters. Center is an old claw-foot bathtub. The tub is filled with bloody water. JAKE is in it, stripped to the waist but wearing jeans. There is blood on his chest. A bottle and knife are next to the tub on the floor.)

Oh my God.

(She runs to the tub, gets in and, after great exertion, manages to push the limp body out of it. Water sloshes on the floor. She feels for a pulse at neck. She tries mouth to mouth, then 5 chest compressions. Repeats. She tries for a pulse again. She tries mouth to mouth, then 5 chest compressions. Still nothing. Straddling him now, she pounds his chest in a fury.)

Fuck you, fuck you, fuck you, fuck you, fuck you!

(She slides off him and leans against tub. To no one—)

I need help.

(Blackout.)

End of Play

CPSIA information can be obtained at www.ICGtesting.com
Printed in the USA
LVOW05s0731301014

3757LVUK00006B/14/P